Cass the cat ran laps.
Cass is on the mat.

1

2

Cass sags.
Cass has a nap.

Zap! The rat nabs the mat.

3

4

Cass can nab the mat.
Cass has a tan fan.

Cass has the fan on.

5

6

Cass has the mat.
Cass is glad.

The rat has a mat.
The rat is glad.

7

8

Cass is on the mat.
The rat is on a mat.